BARTHOLOMEW ROBERTS' FAITH

JEREMY MCLEAN

POINTS OF SAIL
PUBLISHING

Points of Sail Publishing
P.O. Box 30083 Prospect Plaza
FREDERICTON, New Brunswick
E3B 0H8, Canada

Edited by Ethan James Clarke
http://silverjay-editing.com/

Cover Design by Kit Foster

This is a work of fiction. Any similarity to persons, living or dead, is purely coincidental… Or is it?

ACKNOWLEDGEMENTS

Big thanks has to go to my friends and family who read the novel in its earlier form and gave me feedback on it. Your constant support makes me a better author.

Ethan Clarke is my editor, and he's also a big help in finding my mistakes and giving me tips on best practices for writing, even though technically he doesn't have to teach me anything.

If you're in need of editing, check out http://silverjaymedia.com

Ethan also has a novel of his own:
www.amazon.com/dp/B00NP4U6KW
Spoiler: It's amazing.

TABLE OF CONTENTS

1. GOD'S JUSTICE

"Why's it gotta be called *Princess* anyways?" Walter Kennedy asked, his harsh Irish accent in full force.

John Roberts sighed as he relaxed his grip on his mop. "This again? The Lord grant me strength," John recited in his melodic Welsh accent as he dipped the mop into the bucket and returned to work.

The hot sun beat down on the two young men as they toiled away on the slave ship called *Princess*. Other sailors were tending the rigging of the sails, or working with the captain on navigation—which was John's preferred task—or lounging about out of sight.

"All I'm sayin' is we's only makin' three pound a month. Least we could be workin' on a ship with a better name."

John laughed. "So, what would you decree this humble ship's new name to be, Captain Kennedy?" John asked with a mocking bow.

Kennedy stopped working and placed his hand on his chin as he looked away in thought. Roberts also stopped working and watched the wheels in his friend's brain go to work. Sweat dripped off the smaller man's nose, and Roberts felt dampness on his own forehead and hairline.

Since joining the slave ship *Princess*, Kennedy had been equally a source of entertainment and a thorn in John's side. The lithe Irishman's ramblings were so ire-inducing they oft demanded attention in the same way one cannot help but watch a ship as it crashes into a reef and capsizes.

"The *Gallant*," Kennedy stated with pride.

John laughed heartily, his seven-foot-tall frame heaving with each burst of sound. Kennedy was not amused.

"Oi! I should like to see ye come up with something

better."

John gradually ceased his laughter and found his voice again. He wiped sweat off his brow and tears out of his eyes. "No, no, the name wasn't the issue, just the appearance you took while pronouncing it. One would think you were some Biblical character come to life. Very theatrical. Would I be able to see the pose again? Perhaps we can have a portrait made when next we land ashore." John gestured as he peered at the sky and said, "Captain Walter Kennedy. I can see it now." John once again went into a fit of laughter, with some of the crew around them joining in.

Kennedy gritted his teeth as he glanced to the onlookers. His brow creased in anger.

Kennedy lunged at Roberts, but the large man sidestepped, mop still in hand, and let out a breath before a chuckle. The Welshman brandished the mop like a sword, with the dirty cloth dripping to the ship's deck in front of him.

"En garde!" Roberts said playfully.

At the prospect of a fight breaking out, the crew became livelier. A group gathered around the two young men to see what was about to happen. The crew hooted and hollered in excitement.

John was holding Kennedy back with his dirty mop. The lithe man stepped in a circle, trying to see an opening but not finding one. John jabbed the mop at Kennedy. Drips of water flew off the end of the mop and hit the smaller sailor in the face. He wiped his face, his expression pure fury, then pushed the mop aside, pulled back his fist, and thrust it at Roberts' face.

"Enough, you two!" The loud shout stopped the fight and the cheers from the crew.

A man pushed through the throng of onlookers and entered the ring the crew had created. The captain of the *Princess* was standing before Roberts and Kennedy, and disappointment was writ large on his face. The man appeared the dainty

2

sort, with his white wig poking out of his tricorn hat, and his perfectly clean appearance, but he gave a look which brooked no resistance.

"I tell you gentlemen: You are trying my patience." The captain grabbed John's mop from him.

Roberts and Kennedy had the good sense to look sheepish in front of the captain. "It won't happen again, Captain Plumb," Roberts assured the man.

"You tell me again and again you two will not fight and you will work harder, and yet here you are again. If you would not seek to antagonise Walter so, John, then perhaps you would not have to lie to me so much. What does the Lord say about liars?"

John was taken aback. "He hates a lying tongue."

"Correct. Take yourself below deck and reflect on your actions," Captain Plumb commanded.

Roberts gazed at the floorboards as he said, "Yes, Captain," and then he walked away.

"And, you!" Captain Plumb shouted with one finger pointed directly at the remaining transgressor. "I expect this deck to be spotless by the time you're done. You hear me, Kennedy?"

The man's mouth opened wide, incredulous at the captain's harsher treatment of him over Roberts. Roberts was looking over his shoulder with a wide grin. Kennedy gritted his yellowish teeth and went back to work with a "Yes, Captain."

Roberts sauntered lazily to the steps and into the lower deck. He entered the crew quarters, which doubled as mess during the day. Far aft was the galley, and towards the bow two thirds of the ship was taken up by the slaves' quarters.

Roberts moved to the galley and secured some dry biscuits when he was sure none could see, and then headed to the slaves' quarters.

Roberts went through a door into a closed section of the ship set apart specifically for the transport of the slaves. The captives were laid out shoulder to shoulder on the deck of the ship, and every two feet up was a wooden bunk for more slaves. They were packed so tightly there was barely any room to breathe.

The smell of sweat, disease and decay filled the room. Roberts had steeled himself against the scent long ago, and the thoughts of where it developed were pushed far from his mind. He didn't want to think about the dead and sick in the cabin. He felt bad enough about his job on board as it was.

Roberts proceeded to the back of the ship and sat down. He handed his biscuits to the nearby slaves, who wordlessly accepted and devoured the gift, but Roberts gave a more generous portion to one in particular.

"Thank you, again, my friend," a slave at eye-level to Roberts said in a thick British accent. The man was thin and frail, of deep complexion, and had long hair on his head and face.

"It is the least I can do, and unfortunately it is also all I can do for you, Talib," Roberts replied.

Roberts' friend quickly consumed the biscuit. "The least you do is the reason I still live now. Please, though, John, you must call me Bartholomew. If your crewmates hear you call me by that name you will be in trouble."

"I care not what mortal men can do to me."

Bartholomew managed a weak laugh. "Yes, that sounds like something you would say. 'Fear not them which kill the body'," Bartholomew recited. "Please, for my sake, call me by the name chosen for me."

Roberts sighed. "You win, I will call you Bartholomew." He told Bartholomew of what brought him to the slave's quarters and the dark-skinned man smiled. Afterwards, John read aloud a few passages from a Bible he kept in his pocket. The worn leather and curled pages bespoke its well-used nature.

After Roberts was done reading, Bartholomew seemed pensive. "John, can I ask you a question about God?"

"Of course. I do not purport myself to be a priest, but I will do my best to answer you."

Bartholomew Roberts' Faith

"What does the Bible say about justice?"

Roberts was taken aback, but began thumbing through his Bible after recovering. "In the book of Isaiah it says, 'For I the Lord love judgment, I hate robbery...'"

"There. He hates robbery. What of my people, who have been robbed?"

Roberts' jaw went agape as he tried to stammer out words. "I don't follow."

Bartholomew stared intensely at Roberts. "My people have been robbed of their lives, of their family, of their homes. Where is the justice for them?"

"Well I..."

"Are all the men aboard godly men as you, John? Is slavery God's work? What does the Bible say about slavery?"

Roberts' face felt hot. "I... I don't know," he lied. *'Inherit them for a possession; they shall be your bondmen forever.'*

"What sin have we done to deserve this?" Bartholomew gestured around him as best as he could in his cramped bunk.

Roberts glanced around to his surroundings. He couldn't push away the thoughts of what was happening now. The slaves were starving, sick, dying, or already dead, and for an unjust reason. The contradiction ate at him, burned him as did Bartholomew's eyes in that moment.

Roberts rose to his feet. "I am sorry, friend, I need to think on a few things." Roberts left the slave's quarters and travelled to the crew's quarters.

Roberts laid himself down in his hammock, the Bible still in his hands and a finger holding a place in the pages. He opened it back to see the same verse he'd read to Bartholomew about justice.

"So I am a liar, a robber, and a sinner, am I?" Roberts placed the open book over his eyes and lay in thought. *Please, God, I am in need of guidance. Tell me what the truth is.*

Roberts lay in silence for a time, before he heard footsteps approaching. He moved the book off his face to see Walter

Kennedy next to him. Walter punched him in the gut, but it was more for sport than harm.

"Ah! That's smarts!" Roberts yelled.

"And it's less than ye deserve, John." Walter loosened a scarf on his neck and removed his hat before jumping into a hammock. "One a' these days yer gonna put both of us in dire straits."

"Be thankful it is not today, then," Roberts replied, staring at the ceiling.

Walter glanced over to Roberts while rummaging around in his belongings. "What's got you all mucked up? It's not what the captain said about lying, is it?"

"Not exactly."

"Well, come on then. Spill it or I'll tell all the mates how the captain's got ye salty-eyed and pissin' in yer boots."

Roberts sighed. "I've been thinking about the work we're doing. Are we righteous in our dealings with these foreigners, or are we committing sin?"

Walter scoffed. "You must be joking, right mate?"

Roberts eyed Walter. "No, I'm serious. You are a God-fearing man, are you not?"

"Of course."

"Then what would you say if we were to do this to a man from England? Place him in a two-foot-tall coffin, with poor provisions, next to his sick family, and leave him there while they die next to him?"

"Well, there's the rub. You be thinking of them as us. The Bible says, 'Love thy neighbour as thyself.' These blokes ain't our neighbours. We don't need to treat them with love. The rules don't apply."

Roberts rubbed his chin. "It doesn't feel right."

Walter shook his head. "Alright, then, what does the Bible say about slavery?"

For the second time in his life Roberts was loath to speak aloud the word of God. "It says foreign slaves are property, like cattle."

"There's yer answer. God is with us, so set yer heart at ease." Walter laid his head back in his hammock with finality.

Roberts lay back in his own hammock again, staring at the ceiling once again. *It still doesn't feel right.* The man of God closed his eyes and let the ship rock his hammock until he was sound asleep.

The sound of thunder shook Roberts out of his sleep. His eyes shot open, and he forced his body up to full alertness. He noticed Walter was also awake, nearly mimicking his movements.

Roberts and Walter swiftly jumped out of their hammocks, threw on their boots, and tied the laces tight before running up to the main deck.

Roberts expected to see dark clouds and feel cool rain falling on his face when he reached the waist of the ship, but the sky was clear and the sun still hot. Judging by the sun's position, they couldn't have been asleep for more than an hour at most.

Roberts glanced about for the source of the thunder he'd heard, and soon found the father of the noise. Off the stern, two ships were approaching the *Princess*. At the stern of the *Princess*, he also noticed the captain, the first mate, the quartermaster, and half the crew staring at the coming ships.

Roberts joined his brothers at the stern to get a better view. Walter followed closely behind. He pushed past the smaller sailors to the stern railing, where the captain and senior crewmates were gazing through spyglasses to the ships gaining on them.

The captain put away his spyglass and turned around to face the crew. When he did, a multitude of questions met him. He put his hands up and waved them to calm and silence the crew. Once everyone was silent, he addressed the men.

"Be calm everyone, there is nothing to worry about. I do not want any panic. I will not lie to you, as that will do no good. The ships you see on our tail are pirate ships." Those words spread like wildfire among the men until Captain Plumb raised his hands once more. "The shot they delivered was a warning, and they fly the black flag, not the red, so they should be reasonable men. We will surrender and give them what they want. That is the most sensible action, and the one which will help us keep our lives."

The crew murmured amongst themselves about payment and what will happen if they can't send money back to their families. The captain glanced back and forth between his senior officers.

"Captain," Roberts said, speaking for the crew, "if we give the pirates what they want, will we still be paid our wages?"

The captain scanned all the eyes on him, and then cursed under his breath. "Listen up!" he yelled. "There's only one way we can leave with our lives and our wages. No one mentions the slaves we have aboard. We don't have cannons, and not enough guns to fight against the pirates, so we give them everything else of value and they'll leave. Understood?"

The crew were unconvinced. Roberts once again spoke up. "What do we do with the slaves, sir? If the pirates inspect below deck they will surely see them, and the manifest will show we have slaves aboard."

"John, I'll need you and Walter to move the slaves into the hold. It's the only place we can hide them. Let me worry about the manifest. Go on, now. The rest of you, furl the sails and drop anchor. Slowly, mind."

Roberts nodded and turned around, pulling Walter with him. The two rushed back to the lower deck while the rest of the crew set about their task.

"How does the captain expect us ta get all two hundred into the hold? The pirates'll be on us before we 'ave half of 'em in there."

Bartholomew Roberts' Faith

"I don't know, but we have to. I would rather see these people with us than with those scoundrels."

Roberts and Walter entered the slaves' quarters. "Walter, open the hold hatch. Everyone, please listen. Pirates are approaching. We need you all to move into the hold so you will be safe."

The slaves didn't move, as only a few understood English, save one. Bartholomew moved out of his wooden flatbed and rose to his unsteady feet.

"Bartholomew, please, you must tell your people to hurry. It will be dangerous if they find you here."

"I understand," the man replied before addressing his fellow slaves. He spoke to them in their language and told them what was happening and what they needed to do.

As Bartholomew explained everything, the slaves got up and walked over to where Walter and Roberts were signalling. When Bartholomew finished, Roberts let out a sigh.

"Thank you, my friend. Hopefully we can make it through the day and I will snag us some rum to share."

Bartholomew had a troubled look on his face. "I do not understand. What would these pirates want with us?"

"Slaves are worth money, they could sell you for their gain. The difference is, on this ship you have a fair chance of going to a good home. With the pirates, they will sell you to whomever they wish with no thought but getting the best price wholesale."

"You will forgive me if I do not see much difference at the moment."

Roberts squeezed his friend's shoulder. "Trust me."

"I do," Bartholomew replied.

Roberts' attention was drawn to the hold opening when he heard a loud thumping. He went over to see Walter throwing the slaves down into the hold with no regard for their safety, a knife in his hands.

"What in God's name are you doing?" Roberts yelled, grabbing Walter's wrist in a vice grip.

"What's the problem? Ye said it yerself earlier: they're property, like cattle."

Roberts let go of Walter's wrist, shock evident on his face. He glanced to Bartholomew, his mouth agape as he shook his head, searching for words. "I didn't..." He stared at Walter, furious. "I didn't say that." He clenched his fist.

Walter saw the rage in Roberts' eyes. "We don' have time fer this."

Roberts closed his eyes and released a breath. "I know." He turned to Bartholomew, an apology in his eyes, but the man only nodded, wordlessly telling Roberts he understood. "Help me move everyone into the hold, Bartholomew. As for you," Roberts said, pointing at Walter threateningly, "watch the door."

As Walter walked to the door, Roberts helped lower the slaves into the hold with Bartholomew. They worked swiftly and carefully to help everyone into the small space.

Soon after starting, the movement of the ship halted completely. The crew had been furling the sails when Roberts and Walter went below deck, and the ship's momentum had taken them this far. It wouldn't be long before the pirates caught up and boarded.

Roberts glanced at Walter, who signalled to hurry. He and Bartholomew did their best to rush, but the hold was filled with rope and other supplies. Packing two hundred or so souls into that space was difficult enough to do with a reasonable amount of time.

Halfway through, the sound of a mass of footsteps resounded above. Roberts, Walter, Bartholomew, and the rest of the slaves all eyed the ceiling when they heard the sound. Roberts glanced to Bartholomew, and the two quickened their pace even more.

Sweat dripped off Roberts' face and his arms were getting tired. The tension was racking his nerves, and every sound from above took on the noise of a gunshot.

When the last of the slaves was lowered into the hold, Bartholomew walked over to Roberts. "I suppose it is my turn."

Roberts pulled Bartholomew in for an embrace. "Be safe."

Roberts helped the man into the hold, and he saw a multitude of eyes staring back at him. "Pray for us," Bartholomew said.

"Always," Roberts replied.

"They'll be on us in minutes," Walter cautioned, glancing out the door. Then he took a look around the slaves' bunks. "Oh God, what about the dead ones?"

Roberts swung himself around and noticed what Walter was seeing. Thirteen dead slaves lay in their bunks, rotting. The sight and the thought of what he knew needed to be done sickened Roberts.

"We need to put them in the hold," Walter said finally.

Roberts was glad he didn't have to say it aloud and simply nodded as he steeled himself for the task. He walked over to one of the bodies, and the first one he pulled out of the bunk was a child.

Roberts stopped in his tracks, kneeled, and took a deep breath. The sound of oncoming footsteps above afforded him no time for thoughts of grief. The tall man picked himself back up and walked to the hold opening, where he gently handed the child to his people, and they accepted the dead one in their arms. "I'm so sorry," Roberts whispered.

"Hurry up, mate," Walter said behind him, two bodies slung over his shoulders.

Roberts rose to his feet, facing Kennedy. "Have some respect for the dead." He pulled a dead woman off the shorter man's shoulder and handed her to the slaves.

Together, Roberts and Walter worked to clear the slave section of the dead. They heard a commotion approaching as the footsteps made their way to the deck they were on. When the last of the deceased was in the hold, Roberts closed the hatch.

The door slammed open, and four armed men stepped inside. Though they appeared as normal as any other sailor—woolen caps, heavy coats, and drab pantaloons—they were clearly pirates by their manner. The bloodlust was clear in their eyes, which were quick to size up the nooks and crannies of the room to ensure there were no surprises.

Roberts was still on his knees and he turned and plopped himself overtop the hatch he had just closed. "I swear we wusn't drinkin' again, Captain!" Roberts yelled, his eyes half closed. "Wait a… you ain't tha Captain."

Walter glanced back and forth from Roberts to the pirates, his eyes wide and full of fright. He'd been caught unawares by Roberts' ploy and didn't know how to react. Shock and fear stunned his mind at the worst time.

The first man who'd entered wore a feathered tricorn hat, his brown hair flowing out to his shoulders. He was young, but carried himself with an air of authority. The man approached Roberts and Walter.

"Where is the hold?" The man said with a distinct Welsh accent Roberts picked up on.

Roberts looked around, his eyes still half open. "I dunno mate, when ye find it let me know where it is. The Captain'll be glad to know we didn't lose it."

The pirate did not look amused. "What is this room for?" He pulled out a sword and pointed it at the two. "Be truthful now."

"Storage," Walter suggested.

The pirate peered at his surroundings. "Seems a little sparse for storage."

"We sold it all," Walter replied.

The pirate nodded and walked around for a bit. He took his time, casually examining the room as he circled the bunks. "You know, I've seen a lot of slave ships, and these seem an awful lot like slave bunks to me."

Roberts laughed. "Slaves? Too much work."

Bartholomew Roberts' Faith

The pirate arched his brow. "Oh, is that so?"

"Yea, the real money's in spices, see? Spices, as long as ye pack 'em right, will never spoil." Roberts forced a belch.

The pirate turned the corner of the bunks and walked over to Roberts and Walter again. He knelt to be eye-level with Roberts. "So, where did you put the barrels in this space?" the pirate asked, motioning to the bunks.

"Not barrels, bottles. That way ye can sell 'em fer more."

"Ahh." The pirate nodded. "So, why are you two in here?"

"Havin' a little drink ta celebrate our sales. Shh," Roberts said emphatically, "don't tell the Captain."

"Oh, I wouldn't dare." The pirate examined Roberts up and down. "So, if you were drinking, tell me: where is your drink?"

Roberts remained listless for half a second before flinging his brutish hand forward to try to choke the pirate in front of him. The pirate flashed his sword up and lightly touched the base of Roberts' chin with the tip of the blade.

"Now, now. It was a clever ruse, and might have worked if your Captain's manifest hadn't looked so shoddily done." Roberts lowered his hand. "Now," the pirate began, "get up and move away."

Roberts complied, the sword an ever-present threat on his chin. The other three pirates approached and pointed pistols and muskets at Roberts and Walter while the first one turned his attention to where Roberts had been lying down.

The pirate opened the hold hatch and peered inside. "Well, what do we have here?"

"Leave them alone!" Roberts yelled.

"Sorry, slaver," the pirate snarled, "you won't be getting a payday today." The pirate reached his hand into the hold. "Come, now, people, I'm taking you home."

Roberts cocked his brow. "Home?" he couldn't help but utter.

"That's right, home. We're freeing these people," the pirate proclaimed as he lifted the slaves up to the deck one by one.

Roberts was flabbergasted. He didn't know whether to believe the pirates or not.

Another pirate assisted, and soon all the slaves were back above the hold. "Bring your dead with you; you will be burying them soon."

If these pirates are lying, there would be no point in bringing the dead along. But it still could be part of gaining our trust.

"Everyone to the main deck," the pirate commanded, motioning for the others to follow.

The Negroes followed behind him, with Roberts and Walter being pushed ahead by the pirates. Bartholomew slowed to walk and talk with Roberts.

"This," Bartholomew whispered, "is justice." He passed by to join the other, seemingly former slaves.

The words hit Roberts like a sack of bricks. The words pirates and justice did not exist together in Roberts' mind. They killed, stole, raped, and summarily broke every commandment and committed all seven deadly sins according to what Roberts knew of them. Yet, here they were freeing slaves and dispensing their own brand of justice.

"Move," the pirate behind Roberts ordered as he shoved him with his musket.

Roberts walked with the rest of the group to the main deck. The crew of the *Princess* were sitting in the centre of the waist surrounded by the pirates. The *Princess* itself was flanked on both sides by pirate ships. One was called the *Royal James*, and the other was the *Royal Rover.*

Roberts' eyes met Captain Plumb's, but the captain looked away in shame.

The pirate who'd promised the slaves their freedom appeared to be the captain, as he didn't answer to anyone and was issuing orders to the pirate crew. The pirates had several gangplanks dropped on either side of the *Princess* and guided half the Negroes to board each ship. Once they were across, the pirate captain turned his attention to the crew of the *Prin-*

cess.

"So, now the question is: what to do with you all?" he said to no one in particular as he paced about. The sound of his boots rang into the otherwise silent surroundings. "I have a few options, but the first thing I'll do is this: Kill your captain." The pirate pulled out a pistol and fired it at Captain Plumb's head.

The speeding iron ball hit dead on, killing the captain of the *Princess* instantly. The crew cried out as blood splattered on those closest to the deceased.

"Now, the others who wouldn't cooperate," the pirate called, pointing to Roberts and Walter. "You two, come here. Someone give me a pistol." The pirate captain's crew forced Roberts and Walter closer, while another brought him a pistol. "What is this? I want a loaded one, of course." The pirate captain threw it back to his crewmate and the crewmate began loading it. The pirate captain sighed. "Well, I guess I can tell you why I'm killing you while we wait."

Please, God, do not let it end like this.

"You see, your captain told us he was willing to cooperate, but produced a false manifest. As much as we pirates appreciate liars and thieves, we are of course not to be trifled with. So, he was an example to anyone who lies to us. As for you two, you perpetuated the lie, and did a decent job as well, I might add. Too bad you're a slaver; you would have made a good pirate," the captain remarked, staring at Roberts. The crewmate finished loading the pistol and handed it to his captain again.

Just as the captain cocked the gun, someone yelled, "Stop!" The voice belonged to Bartholomew, Roberts' friend. "That is a good man. He was trying to protect us, because he did not know your intentions."

"Hmm." The pirate released the cock on the gun. "Be thankful to your friend, gentlemen. You get to have a choice in your fate."

Thank you, Lord… No, thank you Bartholomew. Roberts' eyes

15

reflected gratitude as he stared at Bartholomew and took deep breaths. Bartholomew nodded to his friend and smiled.

"The rest of you are free to go," the pirate captain announced to the crew of the *Princess*, "as soon as we take what we came for. However, we are short crewmates due to some recent battles. If anyone wishes to join us, they may keep their personal belongings; otherwise we'll be taking anything of value. Do not be mistaken, this life is not easy, but it is not without its rewards. Any takers?"

I can't let Bartholomew leave like this. If these men are still lying, then God knows what will happen to him. Roberts rose to his feet. "I will join you."

The pirate captain turned around to face Roberts. He gave the sailor a once over and then smiled. "Good choice."

2. THE PIRATES & THE PRIEST

The pirates ransacked the *Princess* and took everything of value, even what little spare clothes the crew owned. All they left was enough food so the *Princess* could return to shore and restock. The pirates first piled everything they were taking onto the main deck of the *Princess*.

Roberts found himself on the *Royal Rover* after gathering his belongings. Bartholomew was waiting for him. Roberts thanked the man profusely for his help.

Walter was soon beside Roberts, a pack slung over his shoulder. After some chiding, he gave Bartholomew cursory thanks. No other sailors from the *Princess* decided to join the pirates.

"So, what now?" Walter asked after Bartholomew went to join his people.

"How about you two start putting the supplies onto your new ship?" the pirate captain suggested. "Sorry, I suppose if I'll be ordering you around you should know who I am. My name is Howell Davis, captain of these vessels."

"John Roberts."

"Walter Kennedy."

"Well, if you'll be with us awhile, gents, I suggest you acquire new names."

"Why is that?" Roberts asked.

"And here I thought you were the smart one, Roberts, being from Wales and all." Davis uttered a Welsh curse under his breath before letting out a sigh. "Pirating isn't the most legal of activities. Let's say word comes to your family about your exploits. They could be held accountable for your actions. People search for vengeance at all avenues."

Walter waved off the advice. "My family's all dead, so it don't matter to me." He dropped his pack, returned to the *Princess*, and began carrying the supplies to the *Royal Rover*.

"So, were you born in Wales as well?" Roberts asked.

In response, Davis asked Roberts a question back in Welsh. "I noticed your accent. I was born there, as was my father before me. Whence do you hail?"

"Casnewydd Bach," Roberts replied in his native tongue. "You?"

"Aberdaugleddau. A few days' ride from you, I suppose. Nice to see a fellow Welshman again."

Roberts nodded. The two watched the pirate crew taking the supplies across the gangplanks to the pirate ships. Roberts glanced over his shoulder to see Bartholomew explaining what was happening to his fellows.

"Pleasantries aside," Roberts began, "I joined to ensure these people's safety. If you do not keep to your word…" Roberts left his threat unuttered.

Davis eyed the larger Roberts up and down. "Understood, but I want you to take a good look at my crew and tell me what you see."

Roberts cocked his brow at the odd request, but took notice of the men loading the two ships. At first, he didn't discern anything out of the ordinary—sailors, as any other, in the same clothing as Roberts—but after a moment it hit him.

"So, you see it, yes?" Davis asked.

"You have Negroes, and Spaniards, and is that an Asian on your crew? I've never seen one before." Roberts pointed to one of Davis' men.

Davis laughed. "Yes, I met him on a merchant vessel. He boarded our ship when we were loading the supplies we took and wouldn't leave. He's learning English bit by bit. I tell you, he's a damn stubborn one. There's times I feel he thinks he's captain." Davis shook his head, but wore a smile. He sat down on the port railing of the ship and faced Roberts. "This ship isn't like the ones you're used to. Slave has no meaning on a ship full of criminals.

"I made a deal with some of the men aboard. If we happen across a slave ship then we will free the slaves. In exchange, those men will forgo their shares. Over time, the whole crew was in agreement, so now we use whatever we make to fix the ship and purchase supplies, and then whatever is left over is given to the men. They enjoy the arrangement. Makes them feel good about what we do.

"If I broke my word and didn't free those people, my men would have my head. So, it's in everyone's best interests to take them home."

Roberts nodded, but he still didn't understand how it was possible. Pirates were supposed to be scum, but instead these ones freed slaves and shared earnings.

Davis switched back to English. "Come then, let's move this cargo onto the ship."

Roberts followed Davis and worked with the pirates to unload the *Princess* of its valuables. He was so focussed on the situation aboard the pirate ship, and the state of its crew, that he was oblivious to the awkward feeling of taking his old friends' belongings from them.

Once the two ships were loaded with supplies, the sails were let loose and they headed off with the wind.

Roberts and Walter watched as the *Princess* became smaller and smaller on the horizon. The bad feeling Roberts had about taking his former crewmates' supplies was there in full force now that he was resting.

"Do you think they will tell the authorities about us?" Roberts asked.

"Probably," Walter replied. "We did steal all their things, and Davis killed tha captain."

"Why did you join the pirates, Walter?" Roberts asked.

"Ye jokin', mate?" Roberts shook his head no. "Pirates is where the money is at. Ain't ya heard those stories 'a pirate captains and their wealth? Benjamin Hornigold, William Kidd. All tha pirate captains, some still alive and kicking. Even Davis seems ta be doin' well fer himself, with two ships and a crew like his. This could be my chance ta become a captain meself." Walter wore a wide smile on his face and had a glint in his eyes. Roberts was all too familiar with that glint of future wealth already spent. "What 'bout you? Why did ye join tha pirates, a God-fearing man such as yerself?"

"I wanted to ensure Davis keeps his word and frees the slaves, but now I feel my fears were misplaced. Davis seems to be a man of his word, at least."

Walter laughed. "And now yer a pirate."

Roberts frowned as he saw the *Princess* becoming a dot against the sky and sea, the salt air of the sea whipping at his face. "And now I'm a pirate."

Davis approached Roberts and Walter after the *Princess* was out of sight. "Well, gentlemen," the pirate captain said, getting the two men's attention, "one thing we usually do after liberating a slave ship is have a feast, so why not join us below for some ale and food?"

Walter smiled and walked off to the lower deck. Roberts followed soon after, and Davis walked with him.

"Let's find your saviour and we can eat together," Davis said in Welsh.

Walter, who was ahead of the two, stopped, but Davis waved him along. Walter cast Roberts a sour look, but left down the ladder to the lower decks.

"My saviour?" Roberts asked, confused.

"The former slave who vouched for you."

"Ah." Roberts nodded his head. "Yes, that would be nice. His name is Bartholomew."

Davis' brow cocked. "His real name?"

"Well, no, his real name is Talib. He insisted I call him by his slave name, Bartholomew, so I didn't get in trouble. I suppose now it doesn't matter."

Bartholomew Roberts' Faith

"No, no it doesn't." Davis smiled and the two went down the ladder to the lower decks.

After passing the gun deck, the two went down another ladder to the lowest deck. The smell of ale, meat, and cheese already filled the air, as did the sounds of joviality from many people. The pirates were singing and retelling stories. The Negro pirates were talking with their people, and others were filling their famished bodies.

Davis went to an empty table and sat himself down. Roberts found Bartholomew in the crowd and brought him to the table, and the two sat down with the captain. Another man joined them.

"This is my first mate, Delliger. He's a fresh-faced bastard, but he knows which end of a musket to point at the enemy, so I made him my first mate."

Delliger smiled and went to shake Roberts' hand. "He says that, but we all know I only let him be captain until my time comes. Pleasure."

Roberts smiled and shook Delliger's hand. Bartholomew did the same, and introduced himself to the captain and first mate, thanking them for their help.

"No need to call yourself Bartholomew anymore, mate," Delliger stated. "You're free now."

"With all due respect, on this ship I am not free. Freedom will be when I am with my wife again, so, until then, being called Bartholomew will be part of my penance."

"Fair 'nuff," Delliger replied.

Food was brought over for them to enjoy. Ale, fish, salted meat, and cheese. Bartholomew gorged himself on everything brought to him, so Roberts had to force him to slow down lest he get sick.

"So," Delliger began before drinking from his mug, "how is it you know to speak English, Bartholomew?"

"I was taught by a former master," Bartholomew replied between bites of food.

"How did you end up acquaintances with Roberts here?" Davis asked.

"I ended up on the *Princess* after my master sold me. After my wife died, I could not work the same." Bartholomew's eyes were cast down, his dark complexion matching his dark tone. "But John must have seen how lost I was, and he told me about the Bible and how my wife is waiting in heaven for me."

Davis eyed Delliger, took a swig of his ale, and then stared at Roberts. "Look, Roberts, what I'm about to tell you is for your own good: a pirate ship is no place for God."

Roberts' eyes shot open. "Explain."

"We're pirates. We've been forsaken by God. The less you care about what God thinks about what we do, the better."

Roberts slammed his fist on the table. "There is always a place for God. Always." The normally dulcet tones of Roberts' accent took on a harsh discord.

Davis glanced around at a few different eyes now watching them. He continued speaking in Welsh. "Roberts, I'm telling you this for your own good. What we do, it'll eat you alive if you think about it the way the Bible wants you to."

Roberts eyed Davis. "Then maybe I didn't make a good choice in joining this ship."

Davis sighed. "Maybe not."

The awkward silence that followed was short-lived, as a crewmate soon ran over to the captain's table. "Captain, there's a ship off the bow."

Davis' eyes lit up. "Is it…?" The crewman nodded with a devious smile. Davis put down his ale and got up from the table. "Men, our luck doubles today. We've found our prey."

The pirate crew hooted and hollered at the news, and after taking a few last-minute bites of food or swigs of ale they rushed back to the main deck.

"What's happening?" Roberts asked.

"We weren't here to attack your ship. We were chasing another, and thought we lost it. Why not join us above? Perhaps this will change your mind about being aboard this kind of ship."

Davis joined his crew and returned to the main deck. Roberts stayed behind with Bartholomew. Most of the former slaves also stayed behind to continue eating.

Walter walked over to Roberts. "Are ye not going ta see what the commotion's 'bout?" Walter asked.

"No, I think it's safer down here."

"Safer?"

"Captain Davis said they've found a particular ship they were chasing. They will probably attack it soon."

"Considerin' we're part of this crew now, we might want to pull our weight."

"You go ahead, I'll catch up."

Walter shook his head. "See ya there, captain's pet."

Roberts took a drink of his ale and began eating again.

"They need you here, John," Bartholomew stated.

"What do you mean?"

"The captain of this vessel thinks there is no place for God here, but he doesn't speak for the entire crew. He may not even believe his own words. I saw in his eyes a need to do good. His crew wanted to free slaves, so he helps to free slaves. He could easily seek fortune alone, or could have killed you despite what I said. 'You shall know them by their fruits.'"

Roberts thought on the events he had witnessed today. He had seen two captains of completely different calibre. One sought to conceal for profit, and the other acted to save people he didn't know. *Davis could have taken the manifest at face value, and left with the spoils. His crew wouldn't have known the difference.*

Roberts rose to his feet. "Tell your people to take shelter. There might be a battle soon." Bartholomew nodded, and Roberts left to join everyone else on the main deck.

When Roberts emerged, he saw people running this way and that to trim and loosen the sails to give the *Royal Rover* some more speed. The smaller *Royal James* was ahead by two ship's lengths, and gaining on the ship in front of them.

The ship being chased wasn't overly special, but, unlike the *Princess*, it had cannons. With its three masts, it appeared to be the same size as a sloop-of-war, but it flew a French flag on its topmast.

Roberts joined Davis at the bow. The captain was peering through a spyglass at the enemy ship, and after a few moments he held his hand in the air and made a fist several times. On the stern of the *Royal James*, Roberts saw a crewmate giving another signal in return, and then that crewmate turned around and issued orders to the crew.

Davis lowered the spyglass and noticed Roberts. "Decided to join us, have you?"

"Consider me an observer."

"Observe away." Davis handed the spyglass to Roberts.

Roberts took the device and gazed through it. He watched the crew of the *Royal James* working tirelessly to move the ship faster. They moved the *Royal James* in line with the French ship to steal the wind from its sails. Roberts also noticed men at the bow, and what he thought were cannons.

Explosions erupted from the bow of the *Royal James*, followed by smoke, and after a few seconds several splashes.

"A warning shot, like before," Davis explained. "If today is a good day, they will also surrender."

Roberts stopped looking through the spyglass for a moment and peered over to Davis. "I would pray for your success, but you said there is no place for God here." Roberts chuckled at his own joke.

Davis chuckled as well. "I don't think God would take pleasure in you praying for us."

"If I cannot pray for sinners, then who am I to pray for?"

"Good point," Davis replied.

"Besides, I think God would appreciate it if there was no bloodshed." Roberts looked through the spyglass again, this time at the French ship. He noticed something about the crew's actions, the way they were moving across the deck. "They're going to turn the ship," he declared, handing the spyglass back to Davis.

"Who?"

"The ship you're chasing. They seem to be trimming the sails quite a bit, but not furling them completely. We're with the wind, so the best bet I would give is that they're preparing to turn and don't want to lose momentum. They're trimming the sails in advance so it's easier to pull them all the way up in a moment."

Davis peered through the spyglass at the enemy ship. "Damn, you're right. It's probably going to try and attack the *Royal James* and break the flank by moving to our port." Davis turned to the crew. "Two points to port!"

The navigator relayed the instructions to the crew, and they set about releasing riggings on the sails and making the ship move to port. As soon as the *Royal Rover* began moving, the French ship made its move as well.

The French ship turned hard to port, just as Roberts had predicted. The wind still blew against its sails, but it wasn't pushed away because the sails were trimmed so much. Instead, the enemy ship was able to turn all the way around while retaining some of its speed. The ship angled itself towards the *Royal James*.

By the time the French ship was turned around, the *Royal Rover* had moved to the port side of its sister ship. The *Royal James* was still moving faster though, and would be upon the enemy too soon.

Captain Davis gave another hand signal, and the crew of the *Royal James* furled some of their sails, slowing it considerably.

"Now it's too late for them to change course," Davis commented. "Even if they dropped their sails, the wind is against them. Thanks Roberts."

The two ships were matched in speed, and headed towards

the French ship. They were minutes away from being within firing distance. Roberts could see the French ship better now. It carried twelve cannons on either side, which was more than the *Royal James* but was trumped again by the *Royal Rover*. The name on the side was *Argent*.

"Men, to arms! Ready starboard volley!" Davis yelled. "Have you ever been in a battle before, Roberts?"

"No, I've never worked on a ship with cannons."

"Well, watch out. This is the part where things become interesting." Davis' Welsh enunciated the hard rolling r and Roberts could tell he was excited from the tone.

Roberts watched the ships closely, sweat beading on his forehead. He was terrified, but excited at the same time. He'd heard stories about naval battles, but had never been a part of one.

"Fire!" Davis yelled.

A wall of fire and iron exploded from the starboard of the *Royal Rover*, and was returned by the *Argent* in kind. A few of the cannonballs hit the water and splashed with a loud plunk. Several hit the sides of the *Royal Rover*, causing the wood to burst from the force. Men were sent flying from the blasts.

The noise of the cannons and splintering wood quickly ceased, but the screams of the injured and orders being yelled continued on. After another moment, the cannons' howl was heard again, followed by chunks of the ship being broken apart and more water being splashed into the air.

"They're waving the white!" one of the crew yelled.

"Cease fire!" Davis ordered in reply. A few cannons fired off again, but after another shout of the captain's order, the thunder stopped.

It was over faster than Roberts had thought it would be. The carnage was still everything he dreamed it as being, but it was swift and forceful, not long and drawn out as he'd expected.

"Oi," Davis called, smacking Roberts' arm. "It's over."

"Right."

Roberts glanced around the ship to see the crew helping those injured to one side so they could be tended to. He was glad to see Walter up and about and unharmed.

"Bring us around!" Davis yelled. When he didn't hear confirmation of his order, he repeated it, but still heard nothing back from the navigator. "Jones?" The captain looked at the wheel, where a few crewmates were gathered.

Davis ran to the other end of the ship where the wheel was. Roberts followed behind. Davis went over beside his crewmates to see a body lying on the ground, blood pooled beneath it.

"Jesus!" Davis cursed. The man took a few breaths, staring at the body of his crewmate. "Alright, move him below deck. Heath, man the wheel and turn us around."

The crew replied with an "Aye, Captain," before following through with their orders.

"That's it?" Roberts asked, unable to keep the shock from his voice.

"Yes, for now," Davis sighed, "that's it. We still have a job to do."

Roberts couldn't help but be ashamed at Davis' cold-hearted attitude, and saw the other crewmates adopting the same stoicism. Their eyes told the truth though: the death of a mate hurt them.

God, please have mercy on this sinner.

The ship was turned around, and was joined by the *Royal James* in the same maneuver as with the *Princess*. They went on both sides of the *Argent* and put down gangplanks for the crew to travel across.

The pirates rounded up the crew from the merchant vessel and put them into a group in the middle of the ship. They kept weapons trained on the enemy crew the whole time.

"Where is your captain?" Davis asked.

The captain of the *Argent* stepped forward. "I am here," he said in a thick French accent.

"I trust you know what we're after?"

The French captain peered to his left and right. "I have an idea."

"Lead the way," Davis commanded.

The Frenchman turned around and started walking towards the stern, and Davis followed behind. Roberts stayed on the sidelines with the other pirates, guarding the crew of the *Argent*. Roberts didn't have a weapon, however; he was committed to observing.

He noticed a sharp movement out of the corner of his eye. A merchant crewmate had pulled out a knife and was rushing at Davis.

"Davis, watch out!" Roberts yelled.

Davis turned around just as the enemy thrust his knife at him. The pirate captain sidestepped and knocked the knife out of the man's hand. One of Davis' crew fired a musket at the enemy, and he fell to the ground dead.

With the commotion ceased, Davis glanced back to the other men of the merchant crew. "Anyone else?" Davis challenged. No one came forward. Davis beckoned Roberts over. "You saved my life, mate. I owe you, and I won't forget that."

Roberts nodded, but he couldn't move his gaze away from the man who had been killed. This was far different from the pirate crewmate who died in front of him. This was a man who he helped kill.

"Come, Roberts, you'll want to see this." Davis motioned another couple of crewmates over, then entered the stern cabin.

Roberts shook his head, prayed silently for the man whom he would never know, then joined Davis and the two crewmates in the stern cabin.

The *Argent*'s captain was kneeling behind a desk, with Davis and the two crewmates watching him like hawks, and with pistols trained on him just in case. The enemy captain opened a compartment in the desk protected by a lock, then pulled out a chest and placed it on top of the desk.

Davis motioned for Roberts to join him. Roberts walked to the other side of the desk. The pirate captain set his pistol on the desk and smiled as he opened the chest.

It was in that moment that John Roberts began to understand the allure of being a pirate.

3. DRINK AND BE MERRY

Roberts was in the crew's quarters of the *Royal Rover*, in the open surgeon's section. The surgeon was tending to the wounded from the previous battle. There hadn't been time to bag Jones' body yet, and so the dead man was lying on a table.

Roberts had had enough of conflict and wanted to be away from prying eyes. He had a decision to make, and didn't want to be disturbed.

"Here," Davis said, handing Roberts four gold pieces before pocketing some for himself.

Davis sent the other crewmates out of the cabin with the *Argent*'s captain while he and Roberts stayed behind. The chest full of gold was the treasure the pirates were after, but a quick review of the manifest showed even more plunder to be stolen. Spices, gunpowder, clothes, food, tons of stock to be taken, and soon to be sold.

"What is this?" Roberts asked.

Davis chuckled. "Gold, clearly."

Roberts frowned. "I know that much. What I mean is why are you giving these to me?"

"Consider it an advance share. I'm not sure if the Commanders will allow you part of the booty, considering how new you are and especially since they didn't see you help in the battle. I know without your help the battle would have been more difficult, so I want to make sure you have something to show for it."

"Commanders?" Roberts questioned, a brow cocked.

Davis cursed and rubbed his chin. "That's right, we never

told you how this ship worked. There are two factions on board the ship: the Commanders and the Commons. The Commanders are the ones who make the decisions by a vote. The decisions could be as simple as which port we head to next, or who will be captain, should the men have a problem with me or if I have an untimely dinner with Davey Jones," Davis said with a grim chuckle. "The captain has a vote, and if there is a tie the captain breaks the tie.

"The Commons have no say in the vote, but they do vote who becomes a Commander based on their section on the ship. Depending on how many crewmates are in that section there could be multiple Commanders selected to represent their wishes."

"That is an interesting system," Roberts said, stroking his chin. *Aboard the* Princess *there was no voting on anything. The captain's word was law.*

"We find it works well, as votes aren't hidden. If a Commander didn't vote the way his section wanted him to they could replace him in the next election. The Commanders have to set aside personal feelings to stay in charge, and the Commons always have a chance of becoming a Commander if they play their cards right."

Roberts was still stroking his chin. "Perhaps Walter and I have a chance to climb above our station here."

Davis smiled. "Don't want no more swabbin' the deck do you?"

Roberts laughed and shrugged his large shoulders. "Let's say I've had my fill, and the years have not made the swabbing any more enthralling."

The shorter Davis laughed along with Roberts. "As I was saying, you should keep that gold a secret, as I'm not sure the Commanders will allow you a share. If they do, just decline it this time, as that's probably double what everyone else will get. You'll make yourself look good if you decide to redistribute it to the crew."

Roberts gazed at the gold, this time appreciating just what it was he was holding. On the *Princess*, he'd received three pounds silver or less a month. In his hands now was more than he'd made in a year before, and then some.

Roberts pocketed the money.

The cargo of the *Argent* was unloaded, with no further issues from its crew. Delliger speculated that once the chest and cargo were sold they would have enough to live comfortably for a long while. But he also said that, knowing Davis and the way the crew liked to spend their money, they'd probably be after their next score a week after freeing the slaves.

Roberts went below deck and noticed the injured being tended to, as well as the dead navigator, Jones. He sat down next to the body to think about his options.

There seems to be no end to the conflict I feel today. I would ask God for help, but I already know what the answer would be. 'For the love of money is the root of all evil.'

Roberts held one of the coins in front of him, staring at the gold lustre. *Why should I have to toil for another's gain? God allows men to profit from sin on a daily basis and those same men call pirates who steal their ill-gotten gains the evil which plagues the world. What sense is that?*

Roberts heard footsteps approaching and pocketed the coin. The person approaching was a crewmate Roberts hadn't been introduced to. He was a short Negro with a timid nature. When he noticed Roberts he stopped in his tracks.

"Ah, sorry misser. I'll come back."

"No, no, I should be leaving anyway. Please." Roberts motioned for the man to approach, and got up out of his seat to leave.

The Negro approached the table holding Jones' body, and he removed his cap. He looked at the body of his crewmate, obviously a friend, with reverence. He turned to see Roberts still there, watching.

"You's the preacher, right?" the man asked.

Roberts laughed. "I suppose so."

"What happens affer we die?"

Bartholomew Roberts' Faith

Roberts hadn't expected that question. He noticed the need in the young man's eyes, so he walked over to the table again and stood next to the man. "Well, the Bible often likens death to sleep, and we will be awoken again to have a final judgement before God. In that sense, your friend here is simply sleeping, but can be awoken only by the Creator. That's not so bad, now is it?"

The man wrung his woolen cap in his hands. "Could ye pray for him, misser?"

"Certainly," Roberts replied.

Roberts prayed for a pirate. He prayed for a man he never knew, and never would know, but who was clearly loved by many, despite his sins.

A few days had passed since the battle with the *Argent*, and despite Davis' prediction the Commanders voted to give Roberts a share of the spoils. Roberts followed Davis' advice and declined the gold, asking that his share instead be redistributed to the other crewmates. As the ship seemed to value transparency, the other crewmates knew of his decision, and in short order Roberts was becoming a favoured crewmate.

During meals, many in the crew wanted to sit with him and Bartholomew, often giving him extra meat or ale to drink. They shared stories of their travels with Roberts and seemed to genuinely enjoy his company.

"You know, Bartholomew," Roberts said on the third night of revelry, "perhaps they do need someone like me aboard this ship."

Bartholomew laughed. "Careful, John, don't let the drink go to your head."

The next morning Roberts awoke to a splitting headache, but after some meat and movement around the ship he felt much better. He spoke with Delliger about what he was to do aboard the ship for the day. As the ship was already repaired as much as it could be, and they had all the rigging men they needed, Roberts was to swab the deck. He was also to be joined by a familiar face, one who seemed to have been avoiding him since boarding the pirate ship: Walter Kennedy.

"This remind you of anything, mate?" Roberts asked with a smile on his face as he swabbed the deck.

"Different ship, same shit. Every time."

Roberts kept swabbing, but glanced over to his companion every so often. As he did, the foul look on the other man's face seemed to grown fouler each time. After a half hour, it seemed to build to a head.

"What do ye keep starin' at me fer, John?"

"No reason," Roberts explained, taking a break under the shade of the sail. "It's just that when we started here, you seemed so happy to be aboard. You even said you wanted to try working your way up to Captain. There's a pretty good chance of that happening here as well. Davis told me about how things work aboard the ship…"

"See, that's me problem. Davis *this*, Davis *that*… Ye two're so chummy already. No one told me 'ow it works on this ship. All I get is a 'mop this,' 'scrub that,' 'hoist those sails, Kennedy.' I'm goin' nowhere fast, and that's all I'll ever have."

"Come now, that's not how it works here. So there are the Commanders and the Commons. The Commons can…"

Walter held up his hand. "I don't want to hear about the stories Davis' told ye. Why don't ye take yer mop elsewhere?"

Roberts didn't say anything else and decided to leave Walter alone. *He'll come around eventually.*

Roberts made his way to the stern as he mopped the deck. The hot sun made him sweat, and the sweat falling on the wood meant he needed to work twice as hard. Eventually he was able to get in a rhythm and didn't have to think about anything other than the task at hand.

The closer Roberts came to the stern, the clearer he heard a noise which invaded his rhythm and made him lose focus. *What is that noise?* He stopped mopping to search for the source of the noise. Eventually he noticed Davis at the wheel, poring over several maps and a compass, and fighting with the wind to ensure they didn't all blow away. The pirate captain was uttering Welsh curses under his breath, which was no doubt the noise Roberts had been hearing.

"What seems to be the trouble, Captain?" Roberts asked.

Davis looked up from his work to see Roberts there. He glanced back and forth to see if anyone else was around, and then answered in Welsh. "I'm in serious trouble here, John."

Roberts spotted the desperation in Davis' eyes and tone. Roberts came closer, and he too spoke in Welsh. "What's wrong?"

"With Jones dead, we're down a navigator. I told the crew a long time ago I was good at navigation. That's the whole reason I'm fucking captain, mate."

"And the problem with this?" Roberts asked, still not understanding his friend's desperation.

"I'm shit at navigation," Davis replied bluntly. "I can't read a map to save my mother's life."

Roberts laughed heartily. "Well, you've got yourself in quite the pickle, then haven't you?"

Davis wasn't amused. "This ain't funny, mate. Hey!" Roberts' laughter slowed to a halt. "If the Commanders find out, they might elect a new captain."

"Worry not. You seem to have the Devil's own luck. I've picked up a few things here and there, being on a ship, so I should know enough to navigate for you."

Davis let out a sigh of relief and moved out of the way to allow Roberts access to his maps and dry compass. Roberts searched through the maps to find one relative to their location, and placed it on top.

"Well, here's the first issue," Roberts said as he picked up the map, and with emphasis while staring at Davis, he turned the map around.

Davis palmed his face in frustration. "You're tellin' me I was lookin' at the maps upside-down this whole time?"

"See here," Roberts said, pointing to the top corner. "This is a compass. See that 'N' at the top? That means north. This is how the map is supposed to face," he gibed.

Davis pushed Roberts. "Shut it, ye git."

Roberts continued to teach Davis how to read a map, how to use a Davis quadrant, and didn't miss the opportunity to jab Davis the captain for not knowing how to use an instrument with his own name in it. He also taught him something about how to read the skies. The information was a lot to take in, and needed to be condensed, but it enabled Davis to manage for the day.

With Roberts' help, the ship was turned around to return them to Anomabu, where the *Princess* had acquired the slaves.

That night, the Commanders held a meeting started by Davis. After a while, Roberts was asked to join the meeting.

They held their meetings on the stern of the main deck. The wind was cold and biting, but Roberts' wool clothes helped against the chill. Roberts joined the twelve Commanders, including Davis.

"Welcome, Roberts," Delliger said, offering a cup of rum to him.

Roberts accepted the drink. "What is it you needed, gentlemen?"

"We'll cut straight to it," Davis declared, with some of the men nodding in agreement. "We've voted you to be our new Navigator, in place of Jones, may he rest in peace."

"Hear, hear!" the Commanders shouted before taking drinks of their rum.

Roberts glanced back and forth between the attendees, his mouth agape.

"That is, of course, if you'll accept?" Delliger asked.

"Why me?"

Delliger continued. "We understand from Davis you have some skill with navigation, and Davis is currently Captain. We always prefer to have several people who can do a job so we're not left wanting."

Bartholomew Roberts' Faith

Roberts ran his fingers through his hair. "What I mean to say is: I've been vocally against being on this ship and the work done here. Why would you choose someone like that?"

"We try to be objective when making our choices, and base it more on skill rather than disposition. Besides, a navigator needs to be assertive. You're a perfect fit… unless, that is… you don't have the skills Davis mentioned?"

Roberts scoffed. "Of course I do, better than you lot."

Delliger smiled, as did the other commanders. "Then it's settled. Let's welcome our new navigator, men!"

The other commanders all hooted and hollered, then drank the rest of their rum in one gulp. The thirteen drank more rum in celebration of Roberts' new position.

Roberts drank in celebration of his first ever promotion on a ship. *And now I'm a pirate.*

"That is definitely wormrot," Roberts noted.

Davis, Roberts, and Delliger were in the bilge of the *Royal James*. Four weeks had passed since the battle and the ship was taking on water. After the crew found the source, Davis wanted confirmation.

"See, here." Roberts picked up a broken piece of wood from the watery bilge. "Look at all those holes," he said, pointing to a multitude of tiny holes in the wood.

Delliger lifted the lantern he was carrying, and he and Davis leaned forward, eyes squinted to see better. Davis nodded with a frown on his face.

"So, what can we do?"

It was Delliger's time to take over. "It depends on the extent of the damage." Delliger examined the wood in the dark bilge. "Looking at the surface, it seems we'll have to replace a lot of wood. Until we examine the keel we won't know if we have to scrap her or not."

"Scrap? Come, now, it can't be that bad, can it? It's just the keel."

Roberts looked at Delliger, both of them hunched over in the bilge, and the two laughed. "How long did you say you've been working on ships for, Davis?" Roberts asked.

"A few years..." Davis claimed, crossing his arms. Roberts and Delliger just stared at him. "Alright, two years."

Roberts and Delliger chuckled. "You'd better be thankful for that pretty face of yours, Davis," Delliger commented, "because that's the only reason you're our captain."

"Aww, shut it! We all know who brings in the gold."

"Well, he's got us there. Come on boys, we're almost to land." Delliger led the other two out of the bilge and they went back to the main deck of the *Royal James*.

Once there, Davis addressed the crew to inform them of the wormrot and that the ship would be more thoroughly inspected. Davis also mentioned that they might need to scrap the ship if the wormrot was widespread.

Roberts relieved the helmsman for the final approach west of Anomabu. With the wind in their favour, they reached their destination within a few hours. Roberts guided the *Royal James* just shy of land, and the *Royal Rover* wasn't far behind, steered by a man Roberts had trained to navigate.

Davis told the slaves, with the help of Bartholomew translating, how they have a friend in the area that will help them relocate to new homes. They couldn't return to a colony without freedom papers, and those were harder to acquire.

Davis and Bartholomew moved to the *Royal Rover* and explained the same thing as Roberts and the crew helped transport the slaves to shore via longboats. Soon, all two hundred were on shore, and Davis' friend was there as well, as he had a home nearby.

Davis gave him a great deal of coin, and they parted ways. Bartholomew approached Davis before he departed back to the *Royal Rover*.

"I wish to join you on your ship," Bartholomew said.

Roberts cocked an eyebrow. "Why would you want that,

Bartholomew Roberts' Faith

Bartholomew?"

"Yes, while we could use the extra manpower, I hesitate to bring you aboard," Davis stated, arms crossed.

"I want to join because I have seen something special I have never seen before: people of colour working in harmony with those of none. Also, I have nowhere else to go. The closest thing to family I have is John. I would stay with you to stay with my friend."

Roberts was touched by Bartholomew's words, but still couldn't help but think it was a poor decision. "Bartholomew, this is a pirate ship. There will be battles, and we will be doing things the Lord would frown upon."

"None of these things have stopped you from joining. Previously, you too wanted nothing to do with this ship. What has changed?"

Roberts glanced at Davis, then back at Bartholomew. "I suppose it is for the same reason as you; I've seen something I haven't seen before within these people... Also, the pay is better." Roberts chuckled and Davis joined in laughing.

"Then there should be no objection to my joining."

"What about working on a ship? Have you ever worked on a ship before?" Davis asked.

Bartholomew shook his head. "No, but I know how to cook. I could cook for the crew."

Davis stroked his chin. "That will work. Let's return to the ship, we can restock at Anomabu."

The three returned with the other crewmates on longboats, the former slaves all waving to them as the pirates left.

"Despite my objections, I'm glad you decided to join us, Bartholomew," Roberts reassured the man.

"I couldn't leave you here without being able to repay my debt."

"Your debt?" Roberts asked. Davis' attention was also piqued.

"You saved my life, John, and the crew of the *Royals* gave me my freedom again. I wish to repay that."

"You don't owe us anything, mate," Davis said. "You're one of us now, an equal."

Once they were aboard the ship, and after the announcement of their new cook joining the crew, the men wanted to have another feast. It seemed that the crew drank to intoxication every night, and any excuse to do so again was welcome. They were also genuinely excited to have Bartholomew join them. Many congratulated him and welcomed him to the crew, and also gave him more ale to drink.

"Do you always have celebrations at the drop of a hat?" Bartholomew asked.

"Most of the time," Delliger replied with a chuckle.

"Doesn't it become a problem? What if we're attacked? Not by another crewmate, I mean," Roberts clarified, "but by another ship. With the crew in such a state, we could have a problem."

"Nah, it'll be fine," Davis reassured him. "It's always been like this. It helps the crew relax. This isn't the kind of job where you want to be wound up. Tempers start to flare and things go bad in a different way for us, the Commanders."

"Let us eat and drink; for tomorrow we die," Roberts recited.

"Hear hear!" Davis cheered, lifting his cup.

Roberts, Bartholomew, and Delliger all clinked their glasses together in agreement of the decree. The celebration for their new crewmate continued on into the morning, and the whole crew was incapacitated for several days after.

4. GOD'S JUDGEMENT

The crew were given shore leave at Anomabu, but the Commanders stayed behind to hold a meeting. They wanted to decide on where to sail next after they sold the spoils from the *Argent* and *Princess*. Roberts was recently elected a Commander, and so he joined the discussion.

Captain Davis expressed interest in heading to Príncipe, an island to the southeast which he'd heard was small, but was wealthy due to sugar and cocoa trade. Some of the other Commanders offered a few suggestions, but Davis' seemed the best as the island was not as fortified as others, and made for an easier target. When put to the vote, Davis' plan was chosen.

The *Royal James* was beached and the bilge drained before the crew began ripping off planks from the bottom to replace. They soon found it was futile.

"Look 'ere," the ship's carpenter said, pointing to the bow part of the keel.

Roberts, Davis, and Delliger were all examining the wood closely. A few holes dotted the side of the keel here and there.

"An' over 'ere." The carpenter guided the three to the stern and once again showed them keel there.

"Wormrot," Roberts muttered, dismay in his voice.

"We lucky to 'ave got this far. A few mor' weeks and we'da sunk wit Davey Jones."

"Thanks, Dunham," Davis said.

After the carpenter walked away, Roberts asked, "So, what now?"

"We have to abandon her," Delliger declared. "We can't sail with it like this. We'd have to constantly pump the bilge, and as the weeks pass the possibility of a breach grows."

"This will put a significant dent in our firepower," Davis

lamented as he leaned against the ship. "Well, it's not so bad. We were short on men before, so that won't be an issue anymore, at least." Davis chuckled, but there was a definite hint of annoyance in it.

"Do we have enough to buy another?" Roberts asked.

Davis and Delliger glanced at each other, and then laughed together. "You're as green a pirate as they come, John," Davis said eventually.

"We stole this ship. It'd be a waste to buy one when one can just be taken. That's the beauty of being a pirate."

Davis and Delliger walked past Roberts. "Buy a ship, he says," Davis commented, and the two started laughing again.

Roberts shoved the two of them, and the three all laughed together.

After informing the crew, they set about removing the cargo and all valuables from the *Royal James* to the *Royal Rover*. The whole affair, including selling what they'd stolen from the *Princess* and *Argent*, took about two weeks.

Their business concluded, the *Royal Rover* headed to the island of Príncipe, a journey which itself would take a further two weeks. During the journey there were many nights full of drunken revelry, and with the crew being at full complement it was even worse than usual. Several fights broke out, but the next morning tempers would subside with the aches the drink had brought on. Aside from those fights, the journey was uneventful.

When the *Royal Rover* reached the harbour of Príncipe they were met with a blockade of two sloops-of-war. Davis had had the foresight to change the flags *Royal Rover* was flying to those of a British man-of-war they'd attacked a few months prior. He also wore the garb of the captain from the same ship. *Royal Rover* was settled just outside the blockade, so as not to provoke the ships.

"Those ships could be a problem," Roberts warned.

"Don't worry, we've done this before," Davis reassured him. "We capture the governor, hold him for ransom, and then abscond with the money. They won't fire on us with their governor on board."

"Then, what happens when we give the governor up? What stops them from attacking us then?" Roberts asked.

"We don't give him up here," Davis said with a laugh. "We take the money, tell the ships to stay in harbour until we're out of sight, then set the governor free in a longboat before we escape."

"Seems you've thought of everything."

"You'll pick these things up eventually. It pays to be prepared."

After a short time, one of the sloops sent a longboat with some men to the *Royal Rover*.

"Hoy!" Davis yelled to the men in the longboat.

"What brings you to Príncipe, gentlemen?" one of the men in the longboat asked. He had a tan complexion and an exotic accent to his speech.

"Straight to the point, I like that," Davis said emphasising his musical Welsh accent. "We're here on a stopover before heading farther east. We need to resupply, perhaps relax for a bit. We've heard stories of Príncipe's beauty and wanted to see it for ourselves."

The man in the longboat examined the people on board the *Royal Rover*, and slowly nodded. "Yes, you may enter," he declared simply. The longboat set off back to its sloop.

Davis ordered the crew to get the ship moving again, and the *Royal Rover* entered the harbour.

"The island is so small. Are you sure you'll be able to ransom enough money for the governor?" Roberts asked.

"See those ships there?" Davis asked, pointing to a few ships docked at the pier. Roberts nodded. "All merchants. This island is one of the biggest exporters of cocoa, and to a lesser extent sugar. Its small size means the wealth from that trade is held in very few hands."

Roberts nodded. *Davis knows what he's doing. If he had been born into a different family he might have been a wealthy business owner.*

"So what's the plan?"

"In a few days we'll send word to the governor to have lunch with me on our ship. Once he comes aboard we'll hold him hostage. Then, we wait for the money."

"What about in between?"

Davis smiled. "What else? Take in our surroundings."

After the *Royal Rover* was docked, Roberts invited Bartholomew to a walk around the island. Bartholomew accepted and the two went ashore.

At the entrance to the pier several vendors were selling various foods, and some of the local cocoa and sugar, but not much, as it was generally sold in bulk to merchants.

Roberts bought some cocoa from one of the vendors. Before serving, the cocoa was fried in a large cooking pot. Roberts was told that the beans take long to prepare, so they were already roasted and de-shelled before being fried with a touch of sugar in front of him. The aroma of the toasted cocoa and sugar was heavenly, and permeated the surroundings. After a short time, the vendor removed the beans, crushed them, and served them to Roberts and Bartholomew in a bowl.

"Oh my," Roberts remarked before silently ravaging the beans.

Together, Roberts and Bartholomew devoured the beans in short order. They agreed that it was one of the most delicious things they had ever tasted. Roberts would have purchased more, but the price was high and he wanted to continue his tour.

Roberts' tour was short-lived, however, as the island was even smaller in population than he'd previously thought. There were two inns, a brothel, a bar, a few homes, and off in the distance Roberts spied a small fort which he believed belonged to the governor. A local told him most of the island's inhabitants lived farther inland on plantations.

Roberts and Bartholomew went inland, walking amongst the tropical trees, swaying grass, and chirping birds. The two took in their surroundings with happy hearts and zest for life.

Bartholomew Roberts' Faith

"After being on a ship for a few months, it's nice to be able to stretch and have fresh earth under my feet."

Bartholomew laughed. "I agree."

Roberts realised what he'd said, and to whom. "I suppose you must be even more relieved. You're free, and you have some meat on your bones again."

Bartholomew nodded while patting his stomach. "I do not remember the last time I was able to do something like this without worry. It almost feels too good to be true."

"It is real, as real as can be."

Roberts and Bartholomew continued to walk and talk as they moved farther inland. Eventually they reached an area with tall plant stalks stretching on for hundreds of feet.

"This must be the sugar cane they harvest."

Before they could continue their journey, they heard a commotion nearby. Roberts started walking towards the origin of the noise, but Bartholomew stopped him.

"We should head back."

"What if someone is in trouble?"

Bartholomew let Roberts go, wondering if his friend was being naive or if he knew what was happening and what he was about to do.

Roberts ran over to where the noise originated to see two dark-skinned people, one man and one woman, kneeling before a tanned man. The lighter man, no doubt the master of the plantation, held a whip in his hands, and was yelling at the other two.

After a moment, the man raised his whip. Before he could strike, Roberts grabbed the man's wrist. He turned to see Roberts, the seven-foot giant, in front of him. Roberts released his grip and the man backed up a few paces.

"What is the meaning of this?"

"Do my actions not speak loudly enough? Stop whipping these people."

"And what right do you have to command me to stop? These are my slaves."

"What is their offence?"

The plantation owner scoffed. "I ask again: by whose authority do you speak? I have no obligation to answer, as this is my property and my business. Off with ye before I strike you as well."

"Answer me!" Roberts yelled, the force of which brooked no questioning.

The plantation owner took another half step back, but stopped himself. "These slaves were trying to escape. I am punishing them."

"How much are they worth?"

"Excuse me?"

"You heard me, how much for them?" Roberts said, pointing to the two slaves.

Throughout the exchange, Bartholomew and the two slaves were simply glancing back and forth at the two men. The three did not know what to do, and so they continued passively watching.

"They aren't for sale."

Roberts reached into his pocket, causing the plantation owner to flinch. Roberts held up his other hand as a warning, then pulled out the four gold coins he got from Davis. He showed them to the plantation owner.

"This should suffice."

The plantation owner peered at the gold, then at Roberts. He was visibly confused, and shaken from this sudden altercation.

The wind blew past the group of people, sending notes of the sea and the local vendors' food to them. The air rustled the leaves of the sugar cane and accented the silence surrounding Roberts' offer.

"What is so important that you wish to purchase these slaves?" the plantation owner finally asked.

"What's it to you? I want the slaves, and this is my offer. Do you accept?"

The plantation owner sighed. "My boy, as I said, they aren't for sale. No matter what you can offer me, it will not match my need for them. We are in the middle of a harvest, and I would not be able to find slaves of similar calibre to keep up with the demand. Return in a few months, and we can talk then."

Roberts gritted his teeth and clenched the coins tightly in his fist. The gold hurt his palm as he squeezed.

Bartholomew went over to Roberts' side and whispered in his ear. "I understand your feelings, believe me, I do, but even if you take these two, there are a dozen more you cannot help here, and a dozen more plantations on this island. You will only make it harder on the remaining slaves by taking these two."

Roberts glanced at the slaves still on their knees. Their eyes pleaded with him to keep going, but Bartholomew's hands were pulling him back.

Roberts stared at the plantation owner, his hand holding the whip half-cocked, and noticed something dangling off his neck. The plantation owner was wearing a necklace of the Crucifixion, open for all to see. The idol around his neck a symbol of his faith.

Roberts turned around with a huff and walked back to the path, leaving the slaves and the plantation owner alone. Luckily, Roberts and Bartholomew were not able to hear any further commotion behind them.

Roberts headed back to the *Royal Rover* to find Davis. Bartholomew followed closely behind, unsure of what Roberts was about to do. The two found Davis in the mess drinking some ale with some other crewmates.

"Davis, I need to talk with you."

"Sure, mate," Davis said. He noticed the look in Roberts' eyes, and elected to leave the table and talk with Roberts privately. "What is it?"

Roberts paced about now that they had slowed down, unable to keep himself still.

Davis wore a concerned look on his face, and eyed Bartholomew. "John, calm down and tell me what's going on. You're acting as if me mum died."

"I know, I just... I knew what I was about to say before, but I need a second..." Roberts began speaking in Welsh. "Instead of ransoming the governor for money, I think we should ransom him for the slaves on this island."

Davis looked at Roberts as if he had two heads. "Are you mad?"

"No, I am very much in control of my faculties. Well? What do you say?"

"I say you're mad if you think we can."

Roberts continued to pace around the ship, his footsteps loud and pronounced. "Why not? Tell me why it wouldn't work."

Davis shook his head. "Clearly something has happened to cause your ire. I understand, but you need to sit down and breathe. You're not thinking straight."

Roberts sat down and eyed Davis intently. "Well?"

"Well, firstly, it's not up to me. This sort of thing would have to be voted on, as we would be forgoing money. Secondly, this island has many slaves. One governor is not worth so many slaves. The plantation owners would sooner install a new governor than give up so much."

"Does this crew not want to see slaves freed? I thought that was the main objective on board."

Davis laughed. "No, the main objective is staying alive and living like kings while we are." Davis sat down across from Roberts. "It's easy to take slaves when they're being transported, as it's only one ship we have to deal with, and we have the room on our ship to host them. Right now, we're down a ship so there's not enough room. There are two ships in the harbour with almost as many guns as we have on each of them, and that's not even mentioning the merchant ships with cannons on them as well.

"Even if we can get the slaves on board, we wouldn't be able to escape. It's just not possible. I'm sorry."

Bartholomew Roberts' Faith

Roberts looked away in frustration. For a few minutes he just sat silently fuming. "I want it put to a vote."

"Mate, I already told you it won't work."

"I still want the Commanders to vote on it. I have that right."

Davis sighed. "Alright, if this will help you see the folly then we will vote."

Later that night, when all the Commanders were back on the *Royal Rover*, a vote was held on how to treat the ransoming of the governor. Unfortunately for Roberts, the other Commanders were unanimously against his plan.

Roberts was disheartened by the whole affair, and went to sleep without discussing the matter further with anyone. The next morning, Davis came to see him as he was just getting out of his hammock.

"How are you feeling, John?"

Roberts nodded. "Better. I'm sorry about yesterday. I understand what you were saying. It was a foolish plan."

"Do not trouble yourself over it. Would you care to share what provoked your anger so?"

"I noticed yesterday the conditions of the slaves on the island, possibly even the least extent of it, and I felt powerless to help them. My whole life I've been more than privileged compared to Negroes and I've been blind to the plight of slaves, or I looked the other way. I don't want to do so again."

Davis leaned against a hammock. The swaying of the ship moved him back and forth on it. "I understand, but from a pirate who's been living the life for some time to one relatively new, my advice is this: you must choose your battles wisely. We can't change the world.

"Right now, you're too soft. You'll die a quick death if you keep on the way you are. Know when you can help someone and when you have to walk away. Worry about you and your comrades first, the enemy next to you second, and everything else third.

"These men are relying on you to watch their backs and

49

keep them safe. If you're focussed on helping someone else, they'll die. Understand?"

"I understand," Roberts said. He leaned back into his hammock and let out a sigh, then ran his fingers through his hair. "So, how is the ransom plan going?"

"I just had someone send my invitation to the governor for lunch on the ship. With luck, we'll hear from him shortly. In the meantime I have to dress the part of a naval captain."

Roberts examined his friend's current attire. He was wearing little better than rags. From his hat to his boots, every article of clothing bore some sort of tear or damage.

"If you're supposed to be a British captain, then I'm a saint."

"Hey, I said I needed to change. Clothes are expensive. It's another good thing to steal. Nothing beats a wool cap on a cold ship."

"I second that."

Roberts returned to the main deck as Davis went to his quarters to find a change of clothes suitable for the task ahead. He noticed Walter there, swabbing the deck as usual.

"Walter! Have you gone ashore yet?"

"No, I 'aven't," Walter replied curtly.

"Well, might I suggest visiting a local cocoa vendor? They cook them with sugar and while they are a bit dry it is also quite tasty. One of a kind, a must-buy."

"I'll have ta try some then."

"Well, why don't we buy some right now? Soon we won't have a chance to. I'll purchase them for you, if that's what you're worried about."

"I don' need yer charity!" Walter shouted.

Roberts' mood changed instantly. "It isn't charity. I wish to give you something out of kindness. We are friends, are we not?"

Walter laughed. "We wus never friends. I've seen tha way ya always look down on me. At least before we wus on the level. Now, jus' because yer Welsh, you've become a Commander while I'm left in the dust. Jus' leave me in peace. Play with the captain if yer bored."

Roberts was about to object, but realised nothing he said would do any good right now, so he left Walter alone.

He's not wrong. I have thought lesser of his ideas in the past, and I happened to be in the right place at the right time to get where I am today.

Before Roberts could dwell on it further, Davis walked up to the main deck. He wore a new outfit and new hat in the style of a British naval captain. It was even more convincing than the one he'd worn when they entered the harbour. He was dressed in a blue bicorn hat, a blue jerkin with tailcoats over a white shirt, and a cravat around his neck. White breeches and black shoes completed the costume.

Roberts laughed at the sight, especially when Davis began walking with his back unnaturally straight.

"Oh bugger off, it's the best I could do with what I had."

Roberts waved his hand. "No, it's perfect, but that's what's so hilarious. You look like a git."

"Laugh all you want, this is what will win us the day, I'll show you."

"Yessir, Captain, sir."

"Shut it," Davis ordered, but Roberts still couldn't stifle his laughter.

Later that day, while everyone was having supper and drinking too heavily once again, they received word back from the governor via letter. Davis had Roberts read it to him at their table.

"Hello Captain Davies?" Roberts asked, confused by the first line in the letter.

"That's the name I told my messenger to give."

Roberts continued. "May this letter find you and your crew in good health and spirits. Let me first welcome you to our beautiful island of Príncipe. I accept your invitation for a luncheon on your ship, however it will have to be on the morrow. Tonight I would like to have wine at my fort with you. If this is acceptable, please accept a coach I have prepared to bring you and three officers with you. Signed Marco Espada, Governor of Príncipe."

"Well, I suppose I'll be having wine with the governor tonight. Care to join me?"

Roberts thought about it for a moment. "Wine at the governor's fort... That is very tempting. How about a favour instead?" Davis motioned for Roberts to continue. "How about taking Walter Kennedy instead?"

Davis glanced over at Walter Kennedy, sitting and drinking alone, then back at Roberts. "Truly?"

"Please, give him a chance. He's ambitious and I'm sure if you give him a little attention he'll be all the more loyal to you."

"You make it sound as if he's more a dog than a man."

Roberts smiled slyly, a drink in his hands. "Haven't you always wanted a pet?"

Davis frowned. "Not particularly, but I suppose it will be fine having him along this one time. If he proves himself then perhaps I can find him something else to do."

"Thank you, Davis. A chance is all I'm asking for."

"Right. Now, time to put this getup to use. Delliger!" Davis yelled, getting his first mate's attention. "Get Kennedy and another man in some nice clothes, we have an appointment with the governor."

Delliger nodded, and gathered the crewmates together before heading to the crew's quarters to find appropriate clothes. By the time they were changed the sun was down and the coach had arrived to pick them up. Davis told the other crewmates and Commanders to keep watch while they were gone.

After seeing them off, Roberts decided to have a nap in his hammock. *I do hope Walter makes a good impression. He's on his own now.*

Davis, Delliger, Walter, and another crewmate sat in cushioned seats inside of the four-horse coach as it took them to the governor's fort. If the coach was moving more quickly their ride would have only been a few minutes, but the driver seemed content to leave the horse at a trot.

"Well, at least the ride is comfortable. My clothes feel as though they're meant for a child," Delliger commented, pulling on his collar. "What about you, Walter? How's the fit?"

"Snug," Walter replied. "I find it itches more than the wool," he said, scratching his legs.

"I wonder why that is."

"So, everyone know what's going on tonight, right?" Davis asked.

"I think so. You both confident in your roles?" Delliger looked at Walter and the other crewmate, who both nodded.

"Captain Davies, an' his first mate Delliber. Excellent names," Walter joked with a smile.

"They've always worked in the past," Davis replied.

"Have to learn when to leave well enough alone sometimes. Too many stories in your head and you're liable to jumble them up."

Walter chuckled and saluted. "Yes, sir, Delliber."

The others in the coach laughed along with Walter's jesting.

Suddenly, the coach stopped moving. "That's odd," Davis remarked. He opened the door at the side of the coach. "Driver, why have we stopped?"

Before there was an answer, Davis noticed movement in the trees off the road. He saw people converging on the coach, weapons in hand.

"Die, pirate scum!" someone yelled.

Davis pulled the door to the coach shut and covered his face. A storm of bullets rained on the coach like hail in a storm. The bullets ripped through the wood and fabric, and through the sound of the muskets and men shouting, they could hear horses dying and collapsing to the ground.

After the first wave of bullets, Davis opened his eyes. He felt warmth on his arm, and noticed blood seeping out of a wound on his shoulder, but felt no pain. He glanced around the coach.

"Oh, God, Delliger!"

"Shit, he's dead," Walter said, glancing at Delliger and then at the dead body of the other crewmate next to him. "We're dead!" Walter screamed.

Davis turned to Walter and shook him hard. "It's not over yet, dammit!"

Davis pulled out a pistol and a knife. He opened the door of the coach and fired his pistol at the first man he saw. The man fell to the ground, dead. Davis then threw his knife at another person. The knife made a *thunk* as it hit the man's neck. The enemy clutched his neck and fell to his knees, blood gushing out of the wound.

Davis exited the coach, pulling Walter along. No enemies were on that side of the coach, but he could hear footsteps and shouts on the other side.

Davis started reloading his pistol. "What do you have for weapons?"

Walter appeared dazed. "Uhh, a pistol and a cutlass."

"Alright, go to the front of the coach. We'll fend them off, and then we'll head back to the ship and sail away."

Walter walked listlessly to the front of the coach, and Davis moved to the back. When Davis was just finishing loading his pistol, he noticed Walter running out of the corner of his eye. Walter was running away from the fight and into a field towards the harbour.

"Dad damn you, you coward. You'll rot in hell for this!" Davis yelled.

Davis closed his eyes and took a few deep breaths.

All they that take up the sword will perish by the sword, right John?

Davis opened his eyes and stepped out from the back of the coach to fight against his enemies, as he had done countless times before.

Bartholomew Roberts' Faith

Roberts felt a chill and awoke with a start. A feeling of dread swept over him, and he became restless. The ale he'd drunk earlier had left him a little groggy, but the feeling he now had overpowered it. Roberts jumped off his hammock and walked up to the main deck of the ship to get some fresh air.

Outside, amidst the barrels, cannons, and rigging rope, was Bartholomew. The dark man was staring out at the town in the night. The moon was full in the sky on the horizon, and its pale glow was just starting to replace the sun.

"Beautiful night, isn't it?" Roberts commented as he went to stand beside Bartholomew.

Bartholomew glanced over to him, then back to the moon. "Yes, it is."

"I forgot to ask you how it's been aboard the ship since you joined."

"Everyone is welcoming and kind, and there are others who've dealt with slavery in the past. They understand where I came from, and offered advice on how to live this type of life."

Roberts nodded and smiled. "That's good. The food has certainly gotten better since you started cooking. I'm appreciative of that fact."

Bartholomew laughed. "Perhaps that has helped in the crew being accepting of me as well."

They observed the quiet town for a few moments until they heard a commotion. The noise of shouting people and loud pops floated to them across the harbour. Bartholomew and Roberts glanced at each other to see if the other was hearing the same thing.

Ten crewmates keeping watch on deck also took notice of the noise, and moved to the starboard side of the ship to catch a better glimpse of what it was.

The noises grew louder until they noticed a man running onto the pier from the town. Because of the darkness, Roberts wasn't able to make out who the man was, but he kept running closer to the *Royal Rover*. When the man was within sight, Roberts realised what his sense of dread had hinted at.

Walter Kennedy ran up the gangplank of the *Royal Rover* and up to the crewmates meeting him on the port side of the ship. Roberts and Bartholomew also rushed over to Walter.

Walter was out of breath and nearly collapsed on the deck. "Trap... Ambushed..." he tried to spit out through deep breaths while doubled over.

"Just breathe, man," Roberts commanded.

Walter took a few big breaths and stood up. "Davis, Delliger, Jerome, they're all dead."

Some of the men gasped. Roberts was visibly taken aback. He couldn't even process the deaths yet. "What happened?" he asked.

"It was a trap, we were ambushed. The governor must have found out we're pirates. I was chased here. We have to cut and run before they signal the ships."

Walter's mention of the ships drew Roberts' attention to the sloops-of-war in the harbour. He looked over the water, and plainly saw the two sloops-of-war circling. Their sails were furled and they appeared to be simply floating there, but the portholes on the gun deck were open, signalling that the cannons were ready to fire.

They wouldn't fire right now, they won't risk hitting the town. They'll wait until we try to leave, and then cut us off.

"You two," Roberts said, pointing to two of the men on watch. "Get below deck and wake everyone up. We need the cannons loaded and these sails down." The two crewmates nodded and dashed down to the lower decks to wake the rest of the crew. "Everyone else: get started on releasing the rigging, and detach us from the pier."

Roberts began to join the men in releasing the rigging, but saw Walter still just standing around. "Walter! Get moving!" he bellowed.

Walter's eyes focussed, he nodded, and then went to the nearest rope ladder and climbed up to a mast.

Roberts helped in preparing the sails for departure while Bartholomew kept watch on the town. Light from lanterns crept ever closer to the harbour, and the din of many voices arrived with it.

After a few minutes, the men Roberts had sent below returned with fifteen others. Roberts went over to them. "Why are there so few?"

"Sir, we managed to wake half the gunners and these men. The rest are tanked."

Roberts examined the men that were able to be awoken, and even they seemed to be only half aware of what was happening. "Damn. We can't fight with only half our guns. I knew drinking on duty would become a problem." Roberts glanced at the harbour and the two sloops, and then took note of the direction the wind was blowing. "Listen up; we have only one chance at this. Tell the gunners to load starboard. Once we're sailing, we can't get caught by both of those sloops, so we have to swoop around and attack the one on the left. Then we can use the wind to head north and out of here."

The men nodded, and one went below to issue Roberts' orders while the others helped their brothers in releasing the sails.

"John, they're here!" Bartholomew yelled.

Roberts turned around to see Bartholomew on the starboard bow, pointing to the town. He followed the man's finger and saw men with muskets lining the pier and taking aim.

"Bartholomew, get down!" Roberts screamed.

The sound of a dozen muskets rang into the night. Bullets flew through the air in a dozen different directions. Bartholomew's hands lifted to cover his ears as he started to kneel, but he was too late.

A bullet struck him through the back. He stepped forward with the force, and then another bullet hit him in the side of his stomach. He fell to the deck.

"Bartholomew! Talib!" Roberts screamed as he ran over to his friend's side. He picked the fallen man up and inspected his wounds. "Talib, Talib, please no. Don't die, Talib."

Bartholomew's eyes opened and he turned his head to face

Roberts. "I told you, my name is Bartholomew."

Roberts' legs were warm, and he noticed a pool of blood forming beneath him. "It'll be alright. You're going to live Talib."

"I suppose you can call me Talib now, I think I'll see my wife very soon."

"No, no, no. You're not Talib. Please, stay with me." Roberts grabbed his friend's hand and gripped it hard.

"Or maybe this is God's judgement. Maybe I'll be sent to hell for joining pirates. I guess I'll find out soon."

"No, don't say that, Talib." Roberts heard the pirates around him yelling and more snaps of gunfire from the harbour.

"Thank you for being my friend, John. I wouldn't have been able to go on without you."

"We'll keep going. You're going to live. You are."

Bartholomew's eyes closed slowly. "Goodbye, John."

5. BARTHOLOMEW ROBERTS

Roberts lay in his hammock, staring up at the ceiling of the *Royal Rover*. The waves gently swayed him back and forth as the ship moved in the water.

Roberts' plan had worked. The *Royal Rover* was able to escape by the skin of their teeth by avoiding the pincer and attacking one of the ships as it passed by. They didn't escape unscathed, however; they lost four men, including Bartholomew.

Roberts repeated all the things Bartholomew said to him in his head again and again. *What does the Bible say about slaves? This is justice… There are a dozen more you cannot help… This is God's judgement…*

Ever since Bartholomew died in his arms, Roberts had had a constant ache in the middle of his head. The pain would not cease, and the more he thought on Bartholomew's words, the worse it became.

Roberts pulled his Bible out of his pocket. It had been a while since he looked at it. The worn leather, the bend at the spine, the stale smell all showing signs of heavy use, but it had not been used much in the past weeks.

Is this my punishment?

"Roberts?" a voice rang.

Roberts got up. It was a crewmate of the ship Roberts wasn't familiar with. "Yes?"

"The Commanders wish to see you."

"I'll be there in a moment."

The crewmate nodded and went back up the ladder to the main deck. Roberts lay back in his hammock and once again stared at the familiar planks. After a moment he sighed and got out of the hammock.

Roberts left the crew's quarters and went to the main deck. The sun shone brightly, mocking Roberts with its heavenly light. It was a beautiful day, when Roberts felt it should be nothing but rain.

Roberts walked to the stern, where the Commanders were waiting. Roberts half expected Davis and Delliger to be there, but after a half-second, disappointment and melancholy renewed within him.

The third in line, the quartermaster, Hank Abbot, was the one who took charge in Davis' and Delliger's absence. He was a Northern New World colonist who somehow found his way to a ship full of British and African pirates—and the one Asian one, of course.

"Thanks for seeing us, Roberts. We know how close you were to Bartholomew. We would let you mourn, but we cannot wait much longer."

"What is this about?" Roberts asked immediately.

"Well, we put it to a vote, and we reckon you should be our new captain."

Roberts' jaw dropped. "Why? Why me?"

"You know how to navigate, the men respect you, and you saved more lives than some of the men can count here the other day. If not for your decisive action, we'd be sunk."

Roberts rubbed his right temple. "I've been on this ship for at best two months, and you want me to be captain? I can't… I just can't… Find someone else." Roberts turned around and began to leave.

"Wait a darn minute! Why do you refuse?" Hank asked.

"I can't run this ship. It's too much," Roberts mumbled, and continued walking. He left the Commanders in shock, but he didn't care. All he wanted to do was sleep.

The Commanders held another meeting and decided they would need to find another captain. Because the man they felt was the best candidate had refused, they were forced to evaluate others who just fell short.

Each of the Commanders was to bring forward a candidate, and that candidate needed to tell the Commanders what they would want the *Royal Rover* to do next if they were elected. One of said candidates was Walter Kennedy.

This is my chance, Kennedy thought. *I can become a captain, and all I have to do is spin some lies. They already bought that I can navigate, how hard could it be to impress them?*

"So, Walter, what would you want us to do if you were captain?"

"Well, we lost a lot tryin' ta scheme money from the governor, so we need ta capture a ship for some quick cash. An' maybe we can steal the ship too, ta bring us back some firepower. The men need something ta take their minds off tha nasty business we wus just in."

Many of the Commanders nodded at Walter's answer.

"Thank you, Walter. You are dismissed."

Walter left the stern and went below deck to the crew quarters. He had a smile on his face and a spring in his step the whole way there. He went straight to his hammock next to Roberts and lay down in it.

"Better get used ta takin' orders from me, mate. Yer lookin' at yer new captain," Walter proclaimed.

"Oh? I overheard they were considering a few people. What did you tell them our next move should be?" Roberts asked.

"Told 'em we need a new target. That ransom plan was a fool's errand. We need ta capture a ship and leave the whole thing behind us." Roberts didn't reply. Walter sat up in his hammock. "Well?" Walter asked.

"Well what?"

"What do ye think? Ye may need ta vote fer me. Yer a Commander still, ain't ye, mate?"

"It's good."

"Good." Walter nodded, and then he lay back in his hammock.

There was silence for a few minutes as Walter relaxed and let his thoughts of becoming captain of a pirate ship swim freely. He smiled unconsciously as he thought of the prospects the new opportunity would bring him.

The happiness was quickly shattered when he heard Roberts getting out of his hammock.

Walter opened his eyes and sat up. "Where are ya going?"

"I'm going to meet with the other Commanders."

"What? What for?" Walter asked as he too got out of his hammock.

Roberts stopped in his tracks, and then turned to face Walter. "It is better that you do not join me."

"Ta hell with that. Yer goin' ta try an' convince 'em to make ye captain, ain't ye?"

Roberts frowned. "I'm sorry, Walter. I know how much it means to you, but there is something I must do, and I now have the means to accomplish it."

Walter furrowed his brow. "What are ye talkin' 'bout? Ye make it sound as if yer already captain. They 'aven't even made their decision."

Roberts shook his head. "They already offered me the position. I declined it earlier. That's why they're trying to find someone else to fill the role."

Walter was confused at first, but confusion soon turned into anger. "This is horseshit! I deserve to be captain."

"I'm not disputing that, Walter, but I need to do this. I won't let Barth... I won't let the men on our crew who died die in vain." Roberts turned away and headed to the ladder.

Walter followed Roberts to the main deck where the Commanders were still conferring at the stern. When the two sailors approached, the Commanders ceased talking.

"John, Walter, is something the matter?" Hank asked.

"He's tryin' ta take back the offer he declined earlier. It's not fair, I tells ye. That position is mine."

"Well, with all due respect, Walter, the captaincy hasn't been decided yet. It isn't your position."

Bartholomew Roberts' Faith

Walter grew more agitated by the minute. *Roberts will ruin everything!*

"Please, John, tell us what you came here to say."

Roberts glanced at Walter, then at Hank. "I am not trying to take back the offer you so graciously gave me earlier. I do want a second chance, however. As a Commander, I did not nominate a candidate for captain, and with your permission I would like to nominate myself. If you allow this, I will tell you what I want our next step to be, and you can judge me on the same merits you judged everyone else."

Hank glanced at his fellow Commanders. "Let's hear what you have to say."

Roberts took a deep breath. "Over the past weeks I've been on this ship, and slightly before that, I've had my faith tested as never before. I've seen men who claim to be with God treat other men like cattle, and I've also seen men who were not religious save those same men and give them freedom.

"I've come to the realisation that those who are with God are not righteous, and I do not want to have anything to do with those men. I also don't want anything to do with a God that says slavery is alright, or who would send men to hell for stealing from evil men.

"For the first time since stepping aboard this ship I truly wish to become a pirate and take something for myself. The Bible says to not take vengeance, as it belongs to God, but I say to hell with it. I want revenge on the people who killed our crewmates.

"Fuck the ransom. I say we return to Príncipe, kill the lot of them, and take everything for ourselves."

Hank smiled. He looked at the other Commanders, and they all nodded to him with the same smiles on their faces.

"I think we are all in agreement. Your plan is certainly the best one we've heard. Congratulations, Roberts, you are our new captain."

The Commanders applauded to their new captain.

"Another matter I feel we should vote on immediately is

63

prohibition of drinking while on duty. We wouldn't have lost those four men if the crew hadn't been drunk."

"I feel I can speak for everyone in saying that we all agree," Hank said. "Now, we should discuss the plan of attack."

Walter stormed off, rage fueling his every step. He couldn't stand to listen to them talking any longer. *You'll pay for this Roberts. Someday you'll regret what you've done today.*

The island of Príncipe was deathly silent in the middle of the night. It had been a week since the *Royal Rover* escaped. Only one sloop was defending the harbour while the other was being repaired.

Roberts and nine men were in a longboat heading to the east of the island, the closest point to the governor's fort. The moon was no longer full, but still provided a decent amount of light to see by. The waves were in their favour, pulling them inland with little need for paddling.

They landed the longboat on a small patch of beach and Roberts helped pull it up and away from the tide. He and the nine men moved silently up a hill towards the small stone fort. Weapons were at the ready, but the thundering pistols had been traded for restrained throwing knives held by skilled hands.

The men went up to the nearest fort wall, adjacent to the entrance. Hank moved to the edge of the wall and motioned for the others to stay where they were. He peered around the corner and then held up two fingers, indicating there were two guards. Hank beckoned another crewmate over, took his knife and scraped it lightly against the fort wall.

Soon after, footsteps from two people approached. Hank and the other crewmate tightened their grips on the knives they held. The footsteps came closer and louder. The crew tensed. The guards walked past the corner of the fort. Hank sprang into action and pulled one of the guards over to his helper. The other crewmate stabbed the guard through the throat. Hank jumped and slammed his knife into the head of the second guard.

Hank and the crewmate pulled the bodies back to the wall of the fort and turned them over so they blended into the dirt with their dark clothes.

The group waited a moment to see if anyone had heard the noise, and after they were sure it was clear they began moving again.

The crew sneaked along the front wall, and after Hank checked through the door they entered the fort. Past the first door was an earthen ditch twenty feet wide meant to hold cannonballs that breach the first wall, and then another defensive stone wall in front of it. The second wall had an upper walkway around the whole perimeter with a complement of cannons, but it appeared unmanned.

Hank led the crew across a walkway over the ditch and to the next door of the fort. He motioned for the crew to enter the ditch to the sides of the door and hide under the open walkway, then picked up a rock on the stone walkway and joined the crew.

Hank hucked the rock at the doors. After a moment, the doors opened and three guards came out.

"What d'ya think made that noise?" one of the guards asked.

"Ah, it was probably jus' a bird peckin' on the wood."

"Hey, look," the third guard said. "The front gate is open."

The three guards pulled out their weapons and cautiously made their way towards the entrance. Hank motioned for a few of the crew to join him on the walkway. The men stalked the guards as they inched closer and closer to the front gate. The three of them went up behind the guards, and Hank glanced at his companions, each nodding to indicate they were ready.

In one swift motion, the guards' mouths were muzzled and their throats slit.

Roberts couldn't help but admire the coordination with

which they acted. *These men have done this before. It was the right choice to allow Hank to lead.*

After the guards were hidden beneath the walkway in the ditch, the pirates moved on to the interior of the fort. As discussed prior to embarking on the longboat, the crew split into pairs and went in different directions to cover the entirety of the fort. Hank and Roberts headed straight to the centre, the most likely spot for the governor's quarters.

Along the way, Hank did the legwork. When they met a guard he killed him without hesitation. He slit throats, threw knives, and strangled his way through the fort as Roberts followed behind him.

When they happened upon a Negro maidservant, Roberts pulled Hank back and took over. The new pirate captain grabbed the maidservant from behind, his large hands covering her mouth and pinning her arms.

"Please stop, I do not wish to hurt you." The maidservant stopped struggling, but Roberts didn't remove his hand from her mouth. He turned the maidservant around. "Nod if you will not scream, should I remove my hand." The maidservant nodded, and so he cautiously removed his hand.

"Please, sir, I…"

"Shh, shh," Roberts coaxed. "All we want to know is where your master's chambers are. If you show us the way I will give you this." Roberts pulled out a gold piece from his pocket.

The maidservant glanced at the piece, then back to Roberts. "I cannot."

"Yes, you can. Whether you help us or not, soon you will no longer have a master. If you head to the pier, people there will help you escape the island. Stay if you wish, but if you choose to help us this will help you either way."

The maidservant stared intently at the gold. By the look in her eyes it seemed she hoped the lustre of the gold would hold the secret to what she should do. After half a minute, she quietly said, "This way."

The maidservant led the two pirates through the corridors

and up the stairs of the stone fort in an almost maze-like pattern. She stopped just shy of walking up a flight of stairs, and turned around to Hank and Roberts.

"His room is in the middle of the hall," she stated, pointing to the hallway through the opening of the stairs.

"Thank you," Roberts whispered. He tried to offer her the gold coin, but she refused.

"I do not want the money. Please just tell me you are true."

"I promise you we will free you and as many other slaves as we can tonight. That is the truth."

The woman almost had tears in her eyes. "Thank God for you, sir. Thank God."

"God has nothing to do with this. Quickly, go," Roberts commanded.

The maidservant went back down the stairs as quickly and quietly as she could. Hank went to the edge of the stairs and peeked around the corner.

"It's as clear as a pasture at sundown," Hank confirmed, walking around the corner and motioning for Roberts to join him.

The two walked along the corridor, still careful not to make any noise and watching their surroundings for other guards. It was quiet, which was a good sign.

"This must be it." Roberts eyed two large double doors. "Ready?" he asked. Hank nodded, so Roberts turned the handle on the door and opened it.

They entered the room and noticed the governor and his wife fast asleep in a canopy bed in the middle of the room. Roberts closed the door behind them. Hank took the right side with the governor's wife, and Roberts took the left with the governor.

The two pirates nodded to each other, and then covered the mouths of their targets. Both of them awoke and sent muffled screams through the pirates' hands.

"Quiet, or your wife dies," Roberts threatened, seething with anger.

The governor looked at his left to his wife, and went silent. His wife was still struggling and screaming. Hank hit her in the back of the head with the butt of a knife, knocking her unconscious. The governor let out a stifled cry.

"I'm going to remove my hand. You scream, and she dies. Understood?" The governor nodded. Roberts removed his hand. "Where are your valuables?"

"There is a loose floorboard under the bed and a chest hidden underneath. Take everything, please just let my wife live."

"Noble words for such a coward," Roberts said.

Hank tied up the governor's wife while Roberts tied up the governor, and then Roberts went underneath the bed to find the treasure the governor mentioned. Just as he'd said, there was a loose floorboard and a chest inside. He took out the small chest and opened it.

Inside the chest were gold pieces, jewelry, and gemstones. Though the chest was small, it nonetheless carried great wealth.

When Roberts got up, he noticed something on the governor's side table. It was a Bible. Roberts scoffed. "Alright, we got what we came for. Only one thing left to do."

"How do you think you'll escape from here? We have a sloop in the harbour. By the time you reach the pier someone will have alerted the militia. Give up now and I'll forget this happened."

"We won't have to worry about the sloop. We've already taken it. And we won't have to worry about the militia, we've already killed them."

The governor was at a loss for words. He stumbled and stammered to say something of value before sputtering out, "Who *are* you?"

"Who am I?" Roberts repeated. The voices of Davis and Bartholomew instantly rang through Roberts' head. *I suggest you acquire new names… This is justice.* "I am those you have killed… I am vengeance… I am justice… I am Bartholomew Roberts." He took up the sword for the first time in his life, and thrust it into the governor's chest.

Bartholomew Roberts' Faith

Roberts watched as the governor fell to the floor and his blood seeped from his body. Roberts had never killed a man before, but he felt no remorse over the death he'd just dealt.

Roberts leaned his elbows against the starboard railing of the *Royal Rover*. He held in his hands his Bible, the Bible he had owned for a considerable amount of time, the Bible he had turned to for advice countless times. He ran his fingers along the broken and worn leather, admiring the beauty of the tattered relic.

Roberts tossed the book into the water and watched it sink into the depths of the sea. He released a sigh when it was out of sight and then he stood up straight.

Hank walked up beside Roberts. "Ready to move on, Bartholomew?"

Roberts smiled. "Yes, I think I am."

THE END

OTHER BOOKS BY THE AUTHOR

The Pirate Priest Series:

BARTHOLOMEW ROBERTS' FAITH

BARTHOLOMEW ROBERTS' JUSTICE

BARTHOLOMEW ROBERTS' MERCY

BARTHOLOMEW ROBERTS' SPIRIT

The Voyages of Queen Anne's Revenge Series:

BLACKBEARD'S FREEDOM

BLACKBEARD'S REVENGE

BLACKBEARD'S JUSTICE

BLACKBEARD'S FAMILY

The Collection Series:

BLACKBEARD'S SHIP (Includes Books 1&2 of The Voyages of Queen Anne's Revenge & The Pirate Priest)

BLACKBEARD'S BLOOD (Includes Books 3&4 of The Voyages of Queen Anne's Revenge & The Pirate Priest)

ABOUT THE AUTHOR

JEREMY IS CURRENTLY LIVING IN NEW BRUNSWICK, CANADA WITH HIS WIFE HEATHER, AND THEIR TWO CATS, NAVI AND THOR.

Jeremy's first foray into the writing world was during a writing competition called NaNoWriMo, where the goal is to write a certain number of words in the month of November.

After completing the novel he started, and some extensive rewrites, he felt it was worthy of publishing and self-published his first novel, Blackbeard's Freedom in September, 2012.

After writing over ten books under two names, his passion for writing hasn't wavered over the years, and hopes to one day make it his primary career.

Let everyone know what you thought of his novels by leaving a review. He loves getting feedback on his books, and loves to hear from fans of his work.

Want to pirate one of Jeremy's audiobooks? Visit www.mcleansnovels.com/faith-audiobook-offer for a free copy of one of his audiobooks.